Mary's Treasure Box

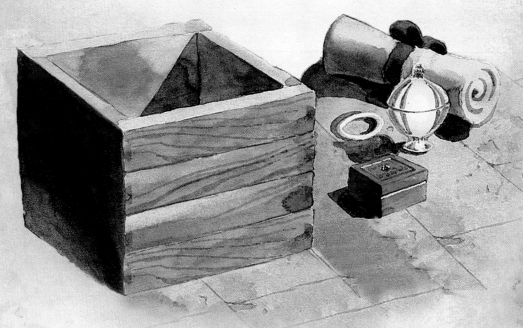

Carolyn Walz Kramlich
Illustrated by WALTER PORTER

Tommy
NELSON

Thomas Nelson, Inc.
Nashville

For Ken and Ryan, two of my treasures
— C. W. K.

To my family, Betsy, Alexandra, Nick, and Philip, for their help,
patience, and endless understanding throughout this project.
And to Linda and Gran, who never let me forget
that someday I would be an artist.
— W. P.

Text copyright © 1998 by Carolyn Walz Kramlich
Illustrations copyright © 1998 by Walter Porter

Published in Nashville, Tennessee, by Tommy Nelson™, a division of Thomas Nelson, Inc.
Executive Editor: Laura Minchew; Editor: Tama Fortner

Scripture quotation is from the *International Children's Bible, New Century Version*,
copyright © 1986, 1988 by Word Publishing. Used by permission.

Library of Congress Cataloging-in-Publication Data

Kramlich, Carolyn Walz, 1954–
    Mary's treasure box / by Carolyn Walz Kramlich ; illustrated by Walter Porter.
        p.   cm.
    Summary: At her granddaughter's request, Mary recalls the events surrounding
the birth of Jesus and the lessons various mementos hold for her.
    ISBN 0-8499-5834-2
    1. Mary, Blessed Virgin, Saint—Juvenile fiction.   2. Jesus Christ—Nativity—
Juvenile fiction.   [1. Mary, Blessed Virgin, Saint—Fiction.   2. Jesus Christ—
Nativity—Fiction.]   I. Porter, Walter, ill.   II. Title.
PZ7.K8592Mar 1998
[E]—dc21
                                                                                    98-6487
                                                                                       CIP
                                                                                        AC

Printed in the United States of America
98 99 00 01 02 03 04 QPH 9 8 7 6 5 4 3 2 1

Editor's Note: The affectionate term *Mammē* (pronounced *mä-mā*,
with the accent on the first syllable) was first used for mother.
It later (2 Timothy 1:5) also came to mean *grandmother*, which is
how Sarah uses the word in *Mary's Treasure Box*.

Every mother has a Treasure Box

of bonnets, blankets, trinkets, and toys,

if not hidden in a closet or an attic,

then tucked away in a corner of her heart.

Mary hid these things
in her heart.

LUKE 2:19

The sunset skies over Nazareth painted a pastel picture on the horizon. The air was cool, and the villagers were making their way home.

"Mammē, I've put the sheep in their pen. Is there anything else I can do for you?"

Mammē, which is what Sarah called her grandmother Mary, lived alone. "Yes," she said. "Come sit here next to me by the fire."

Sarah hurried over to sit next to her grandmother. "I like spending the night with you, Mammē," Sarah confided.

"I love having you here," replied Mammē Mary. "After supper, I'll tell you a story."

Later, Sarah helped her grandmother
clear away the supper dishes. Then once
again they sat by the fire.

"Mammē," began Sarah, the crackling
of the fire the only other sound that broke
the stillness of the night. "Tell me again
the story of your trip to Bethlehem."

"Ah, you love to hear about Jesus' birth, don't you? Well, how about if we—"

"Open the Treasure Box!" exclaimed Sarah.

"Yes. Let's see what we can learn from the Treasure Box tonight," replied Mammē Mary.

Sarah ran to the corner of the room where an old wooden box sat. She pushed the box to the center of the floor. It was not heavy, but Sarah did not want to drop it or spill its special contents.

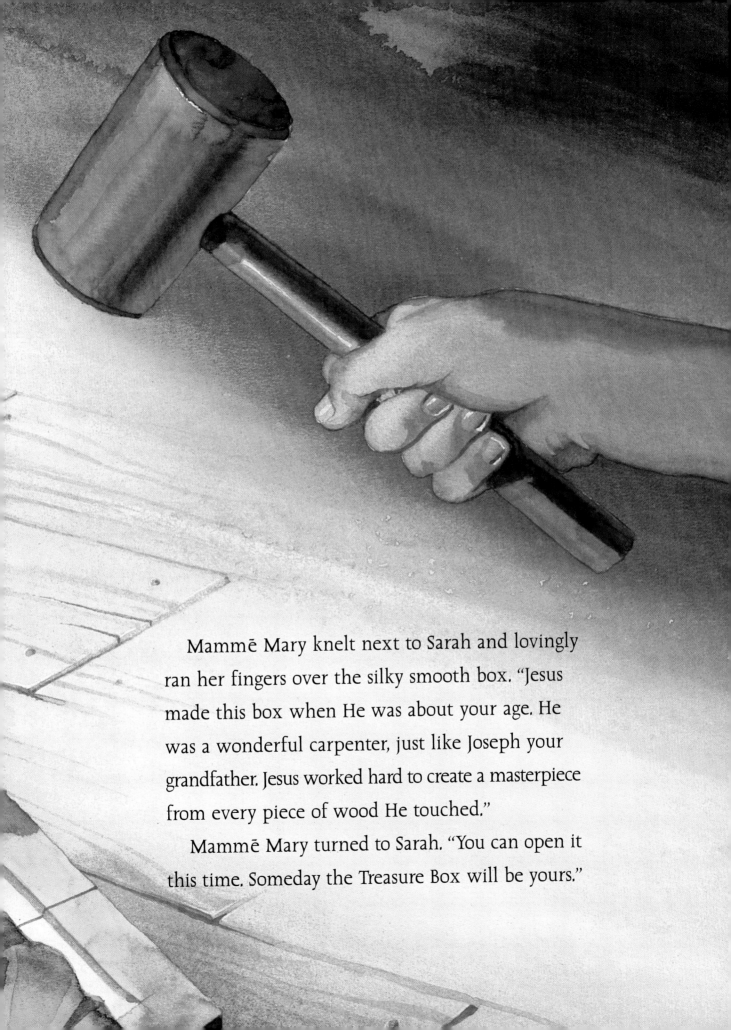

Mammē Mary knelt next to Sarah and lovingly ran her fingers over the silky smooth box. "Jesus made this box when He was about your age. He was a wonderful carpenter, just like Joseph your grandfather. Jesus worked hard to create a masterpiece from every piece of wood He touched."

Mammē Mary turned to Sarah. "You can open it this time. Someday the Treasure Box will be yours."

The young girl smiled proudly. Jesus' brother, James, was her father, and Sarah had always felt especially close to her grandmother.

Sarah carefully lifted the wooden lid from the box. A sweet aroma filled the air. Ever so gently, Sarah removed a small bundle rolled up in a yellowing cloth. She placed the bundle on the floor and carefully unrolled the material. "Tell me about these, Mammē."

"It has been more than forty years now," said Mammē Mary, "but it seems like yesterday. Every time I look in my Treasure Box, I learn something new."

Sarah picked up a little bit of straw and gave it to Mammē Mary, who rolled the straw between her fingers.

"This is some straw from the manger bed," recited Sarah. She knew every item by heart. "What can we learn from this, Mammē?"

"We learn humility. When Joseph and I arrived in
Bethlehem that night, we were cold and tired. I knew that
it was almost time for Jesus to be born, but we could not
find a place to stay for the night. We ended up in a simple
stable, amid the animals. Jesus was born that night. Joseph
piled mounds of this straw in the feed trough and made a
bed for baby Jesus."

Sarah touched some gray wool that had been formed
into a small, cushiony ball. "And what about this wool?"

"Oh!" Mammē Mary's eyes twinkled. "Shepherds from
the hillside came to visit that night, and they gave us
a bag of soft wool.

"Their gift teaches us kindness. Those shepherds had no riches or jewels. They gave generously of what they had. The stable was much more comfortable after that!" Mammē Mary laughed as she remembered that night long ago.

"And this?" Sarah held a wooden flute to her lips. Sweet notes filled the room.

"This," mused Mammē Mary, "belonged to one of the shepherds. When he played softly on his flute that night, Jesus looked up at him and cooed. From the music of the flute, we learn joy. That was the most joyous night of my life."

Mammē Mary picked up the once rough cloth, now softened by age, and held it to her cheek. "The first time I held baby Jesus, I wrapped him up nice and warm in this swaddling cloth," she said, turning to Sarah. "It teaches us love—love of mother and child, of father and son, of God and man."

Mammē Mary spread out the cloth, and Sarah placed
the straw, wool, and flute upon it. Gently, Sarah rolled them
up together again. Then she peered into the Treasure Box.
"Here are the gifts of the Magi."

"Yes," said Mammē Mary, "The Wise Men from the East.
I'll never forget their finery, the most beautiful I've ever
seen. They came to visit Jesus months later, for they sought
the greatest King of all!"

Sarah picked up a small gold bracelet, too small to fit her own slender arm, but it was the right size to fit the small arm of an infant boy. "Pure gold," she said. "Fit for a King!"

"From this gold we learn of purity," said Mammē Mary. "Jesus was God's only Son, and His purity was evident in all He did and thought."

Sarah lifted the lid of a small wooden box and whiffed the sweet fragrance. "Frankincense! What do we learn from this?" she asked Mammē Mary.

"Frankincense is a symbol of prayer and worship and devotion," said Mammē Mary. "Jesus worshiped His heavenly Father in spirit and in truth. I have learned so much from Him. My devotion to God has grown since Jesus came into my life."

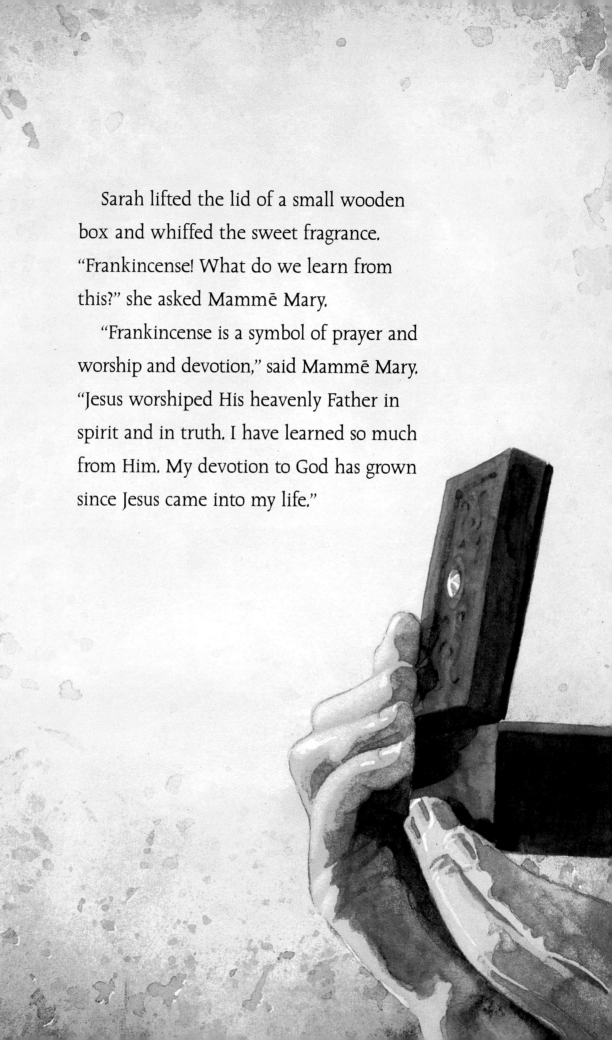

The Treasure Box was almost empty. Sarah lifted one final object from the corner of the box. "Isn't this myrrh?" asked Sarah.

"Yes, the last gift of the Magi . . . myrrh."

"I thought that myrrh is sometimes used to anoint the dead," Sarah said. "What a strange gift to give a baby."

"Not so strange a gift for One who would die for His people," Mammē Mary explained.

"Mammē, why is there so much myrrh but only a little gold and frankincense?"

"What you see is all that is left, my dear Sarah. Remember what I told you about how Joseph and I had to take Jesus and flee to Egypt?"

"Yes, King Herod wanted to kill Jesus."

"We used most of the gold to survive when we were in Egypt. This little bracelet is the only thing left."

"And the frankincense?" questioned Sarah.

"We used the frankincense in our worship on holy days. But I never had a chance to use this myrrh," mused Mammē Mary.

Sarah knew what her grandmother meant. Many times she had heard the story of how the women had gone to the tomb to anoint Jesus' body, but He was not there!

Quietly Sarah asked, "What can we learn from myrrh?"
Smiling, Mammē Mary raised her hands to heaven and
proclaimed, "Hope for eternal life!"

Sarah hugged her grandmother. As their cheeks met, Sarah asked, "Does the Treasure Box make you miss Him, Mammē?"

Mammē Mary smiled. "Oh no, dear! The Treasure Box brings Jesus closer. I know why He came to Earth and why He had to die. He lives here still, forever," said Mammē Mary, pointing to her heart.

"It is time for bed now," said Mammē Mary, hugging Sarah close.

As they rolled out her bed, Sarah asked, "Will you sing me a song first? I love it when you sing about Bethlehem."

As Sarah closed her eyes, Mammē Mary softly sang,

In Bethlehem, a child was born,
In Bethlehem, one night.
To Earth He came, Rose of Sharon,
King of heaven, Son of Light.

And Mary sang and the angels smiled,
For Jesus was His name.
Joseph prayed and the shepherds bowed,
For the world was not the same.

In Bethlehem, a child was born.
In Bethlehem, the start.
But Jesus lives, Rose of Sharon,
In the Bethlehem,
    in the Bethlehem
        of my heart.

In the still darkness of the Nazareth night, Mammē Mary leaned over, kissed Sarah, and covered her with a woolen shawl. Then Mary knelt to fill her Treasure Box again.

As she placed the lid on the box, she smiled, for Mary treasured all these things and pondered them in her heart.